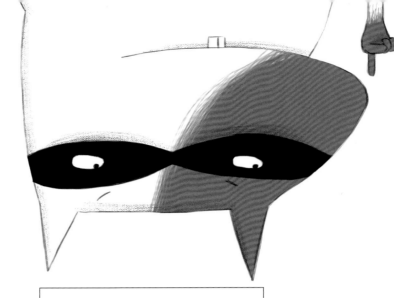

....уууууууууs

For David, Rhian, Wayne and whoever is about to enjoy this book!

JANETTA OTTER-BARRY BOOKS

Bob and Rob copyright © Frances Lincoln Limited 2013
Text and illustrations copyright © Sue Pickford 2013

The right of Sue Pickford to be identified as the author and illustrator of this work has been asserted by her in accordance with the Copyright, Designs and Patents Act, 1988 (United Kingdom).

First published in Great Britain in 2013 and in the USA in 2014 by Frances Lincoln Children's Books, 4 Torriano Mews, Torriano Avenue, London NW5 2RZ
www.franceslincoln.com

A catalogue record for this book is available from the British Library.

ISBN 978-1-84780-343-6

Illustrated with pencil, acrylic and digital media

Printed in Shenzhen, Guangdong, China by
C&C Offset Printing in April, 2013

9 8 7 6 5 4 3 2 1

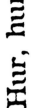

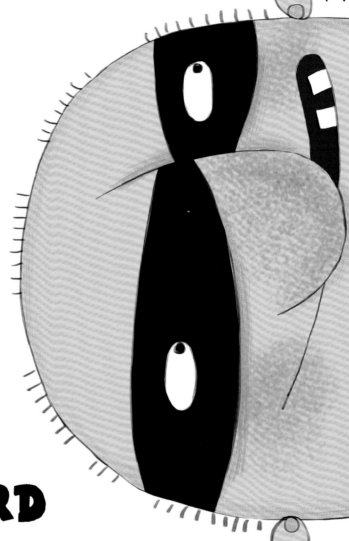

Hur, hur!

BOB AND ROB

SUE PICKFORD

F

FRANCES LINCOLN
CHILDREN'S BOOKS

Rob loved anything shiny, expensive and preferably stolen. Because he was a burglar and he was bad! Really BAD! He was so bad that he liked to:

Bob was Rob's dog, and he didn't do any of these things because he was good. **Really GOOD!**

He ironed,

he helped old ladies cross the road,

and he baked the most *spectacular* cakes.

And he was taught by his mum always to be faithful to his owner.

Yes, even if he **was** a burglar.

Every evening when the sun went down, Bob and Rob put on their masks and set off to find loot.

But Rob wasn't just bad, he was a bad burglar too.

Bob was sad, but he decided to forget his dreams of ever becoming a normal dog. After all, he had to remain faithful to his owner, even if he **was** a burglar.

Then one night, while out on the prowl, Bob and Rob spotted a **huge** pile of presents. And what's more, the window was open.

"Hey, talk about easy pickings!" sniggered Rob. "Keep an eye out while I grab this lot."

So while Bob kept guard, Rob stuffed the whole lot into his sack as quickly as he could.

Then they both scurried off into the darkness.

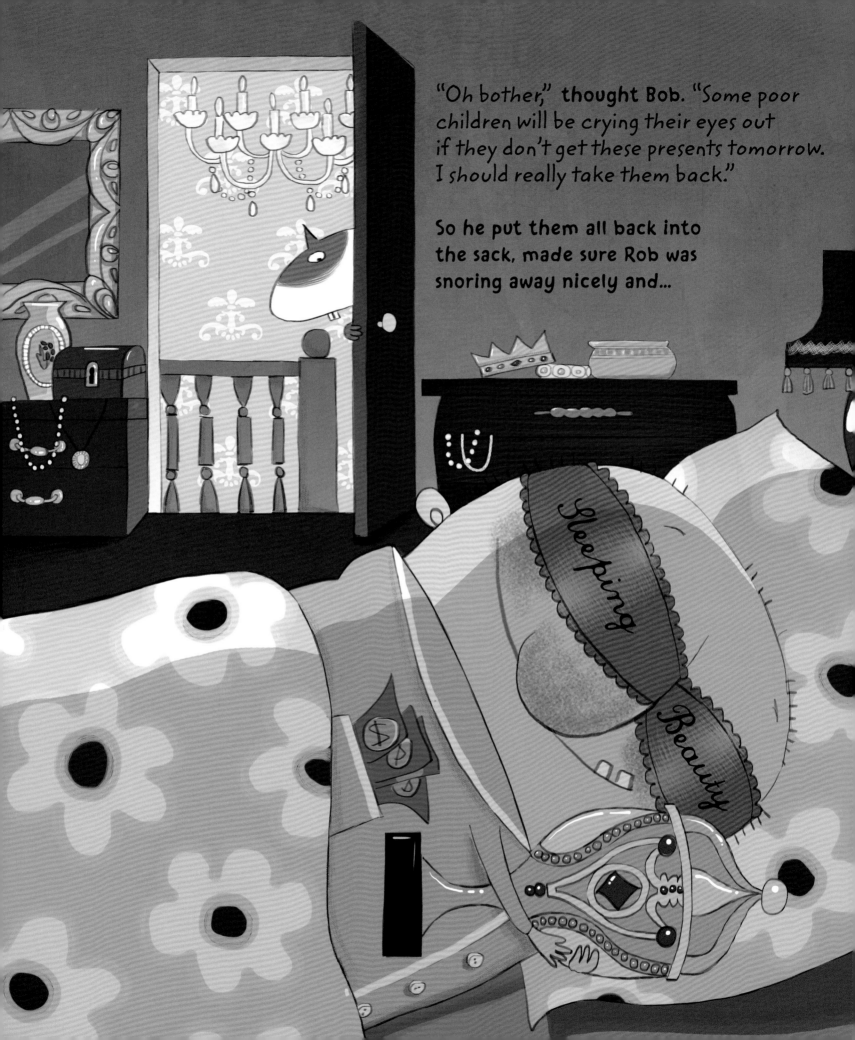

"Oh bother," thought Bob. "Some poor children will be crying their eyes out if they don't get these presents tomorrow. I should really take them back."

So he put them all back into the sack, made sure Rob was snoring away nicely and...

heaved them back to where they came from,
huffing and puffing the whole three miles.

HOOT
HOOT
HOOT!

He crept through the window and unloaded all the toys carefully, one by one. But by the time he'd finished, he was so tired that he fell asleep on the spot.

Early next morning he was woken
by a tight **squeeze** round his neck.

Acgghhh...

"Oh no, sorry Rob, please stop!" he choked,
thinking Rob had found him and was trying
to strangle him. "I can explain everything,
honest...acghh!"

Then he saw the faces of three small children.
They were all trying to hug him at once.

"Oh, Mummy,
this is the
best present
ever!

Can we
keep him?
PLEASE!"

"Well, if no one comes to claim him,
then yes, of course!" said Mum.

HOUND FOUND
Very well behaved!
call: 088 088 088

That day posters were stuck on to every tree in the neighbourhood.

"Hmmm, he sure is the spitting image of Bob but he can't be, because he looks too GOOD!" grumbled Rob.

So

no one

came

to

get

him.

Bob was very happy.
He was never bad again.

And neither was Rob.

(Well, not for a while anyway!)